WHO Designs Zoos?

Dear Reader

We all love zoos. They're amazing places where we can see animals up close, smell animals up close and learn more about them … up close!

But who designs zoos?

CHARLES MAYES HAS BEEN DESIGNING ZOOS FOR OVER 20 YEARS. HIS FRIENDS CALL HIM CHUCK.

Chuck and his team are some of the best zoo designers in the world. They are based in Seattle, Washington, USA.

I live in Australia so I had to interview Chuck by phone. One of our phone interviews between Seattle and Australia lasted for almost three hours!

I hope you enjoy reading about some of the zoos and aquariums that Chuck and his team designed.

Sharon Parsons

My sincere thanks to the following people for their time, information, images and enthusiasm for this book:

Chuck Mayes and the team at Portico Group, Seattle, USA;

Jan Mayes, Seattle, USA.

Contents

WHO Designs Zoos?

1 Designers of Zoos and Aquariums

Meet a Zoo Designer

Chuck Mayes is a zoo designer who lives in Seattle, USA. He has been designing zoos and aquariums for many years.

Before he could design zoos, Chuck had to study many subjects at university. Two of the subjects that Chuck studied were science and architecture. Science helped Chuck to learn a lot about animals. Architecture helped him to draw and design zoos, aquariums, museum exhibits, parks and playgrounds.

Chuck supervises construction work for the Pachyderm Forest exhibit at the Los Angeles Zoo.

CHUCK TODAY

Chuck works in an office with staff who perform many kinds of jobs – from creating designs to construction to landscaping. But he also enjoys stepping out of the office to visit zoo sites under construction.

PACHYDERMS

Pachyderm animals include the elephant, rhinoceros and hippopotamus. The term "pachyderm" means "thick-skinned".

WHY IS **DESIGNING ZOOS** A GREAT JOB?

Chuck says, "I love my job because we create homes for animals in many kinds of zoos."

"We design homes where animals are stimulated by lots of things to see and do. They are fed well and protected from predators. Most animals live longer in zoos than in the wild," says Chuck.

Chuck enjoys seeing the looks of amazement on people's faces at the zoo. At this aquarium, people are amazed by the playful sea otters.

SEA OTTERS

Sea otters are the smallest marine mammals in the Northern Hemisphere. Some of its human threats in the wild are overfishing, oil spills and poaching.

Chuck's team created the Rainforest Exhibit at Woodland Park Zoo, Seattle, USA for threatened species, such as the blue poison-arrow frog.

A POISON FROG

The tiny, blue poison-arrow frog is important in a South American rainforest ecosystem. Two threats to its survival in the wild are the logging of rainforest trees and forest burn-offs.

2 Designing a Zoo on a Hill

Research First

Chuck and his team do a lot of research and planning before they start designing animal exhibits at a new zoo. They will also ask the zoo staff questions about what they want in the zoo.

A plan of the zoo on a hill. It was built around the existing trees, river and lakes.

A ZOO SITE AND ANIMALS

When planning a new zoo, the zoo designers need to see how much space there is for the animal enclosures and exhibits. They prefer to design the zoo around the existing environment.

Chuck and his team learn about the animals that will be in each part of the new zoo. They ask scientists and animal experts to help them, too.

A zoo designer's sketch for a zoo's entrance. Zoo staff will check this sketch before the plans are drawn up.

FEEDING AREA

One important consideration for the design team is to see where the animals can be fed, how they will be fed and when they need to be fed.

WATER AND SEWERAGE

The zoo design team need to find out where the water supply will come from and where it is needed in each enclosure. They also find out where the zoo's sewerage pipes are so they can hook up the pipes to the enclosures and exhibits.

ELECTRICITY OR NATURAL LIGHT?

Animal enclosures need power for lights and heating. The zoo designers observe where the sun shines during the day and in each season. Where possible, they use the sun for light and heating.

3 Designing for Animals' Special Needs

What's in a View?

Chuck's team aim to design zoo enclosures that suit the animals' special needs. One aim is to make sure the enclosure provides many lines of views for the animals.

The sea otter has three views: above the water, under the water and a secret viewing place that we can't see!

MOUNTAIN GOATS

Mountain goats are only found in North America. They are the world's largest high-altitude mammal. In the wild they can live up to 12 to 15 years. In a zoo they can live up to 16 to 20 years.

A mountain goat enjoys the view from its high, rocky environment.

Jaguars are solitary animals. Gordo the jaguar has found a place to hide at his cove in the tropical rainforest exhibit at the Woodland Park Zoo, USA.

Re-Create an Environment

Chuck and his team always aim to design enclosures with features similar to the animals' natural environment.

A GRIZZLY'S ENVIRONMENT

Chuck and his team created the Russia's Grizzly Coast exhibit at the Minnesota Zoo, in the USA. The climate in Minnesota is also similar to the climate in the environment in far east Russia.

For the new Russia's Grizzly Coast exhibit, Chuck wanted the big brown bears to live near streams filled with fish. This allowed the bears to hunt for their own fish, just like they do in the wild. But the fish have homes in the streams, too – so they can hide from the bears!

Chuck's team won an award for their Russia's Grizzly Coast exhibit. They created a rugged, rocky wilderness exhibit where grizzly bears live in a natural environment.

Bears have time to be playful in their natural environment, too!

Life Science

Brown Bears

Brown bears are also known as grizzly bears. About a third of the world's brown bears live in Russia's far east, in places such as Kamchatka. Although they are very large animals, they can still outrun people!

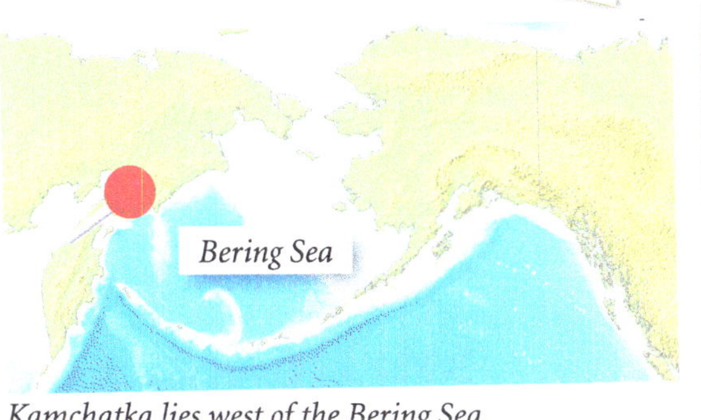

Kamchatka lies west of the Bering Sea.

4 An Australian Zoo in the USA

Look, it's a Wallaby!

Many children in the USA can't travel to Australia, so Chuck and his team were asked to design a children's zoo with lots of Australian features, such as a Wallaby Walkabout, a Kookaburra Windmill and a Billabong Fountain.

a tammar wallaby having a snack

Physical Science

What's a Billabong?

Billabongs are stagnant lakes that form part of a waterway such as a river, and are common in rural parts of Australia. "Billa" means "river", and "bong" means "dead".

Billabongs are important in an ecosystem as they are home to thousands of species – fish, plants, algae, insects and more.

a billabong at the Flinders Ranges National Park, South Australia

Enter Wallaroo Station

This early sketch shows a layout for Wallaroo Station, an Australian exhibit. It is part of the Florida Zoo in the USA.

inside the entrance at Wallaroo Station

Water, Water Everywhere!

At Wallaroo Station, children and their families can cool off in the Billabong Fountain, a water play area.

Cooling down at the zoo!

"Hey, Mr Tortoise, I just want to talk!"

5 A New Home for Cockroaches

A **Madagascar Hissing Cockroach** Exhibit

Chuck and his team created one of the world's largest cockroach exhibits for about 9000 cockroaches at a zoo in Chicago, USA.

AFRICA

MADAGASCAR

The Exhibit's Design

In the wild, Madagascar cockroaches can be found in rotting trees, logs and among leaves. So Chuck's team designed an artificial rotted tree that was cut in half so people could see inside it.

Glass was put inside the tree for the cockroaches to climb up. They are good climbers – even up glass!

Touch a Cockroach!

Many plastic cockroach models were glued on the visitor's side of the glass for people to touch.

THE MADAGASCAR HISSING COCKROACH

This type of cockroach comes from Madagascar. It is called a hissing cockroach because of the loud hissing sound it makes – it can be heard up to four metres away.

The hiss is the sound of air being exhaled through its breathing tubes called "spiracles". The cockroaches hiss when they fight, mate or are alarmed.

Thousands of Cockroaches

Imagine designing a new home for about 9000 large Madagascar hissing cockroaches – each measuring up to ten centimetres long!

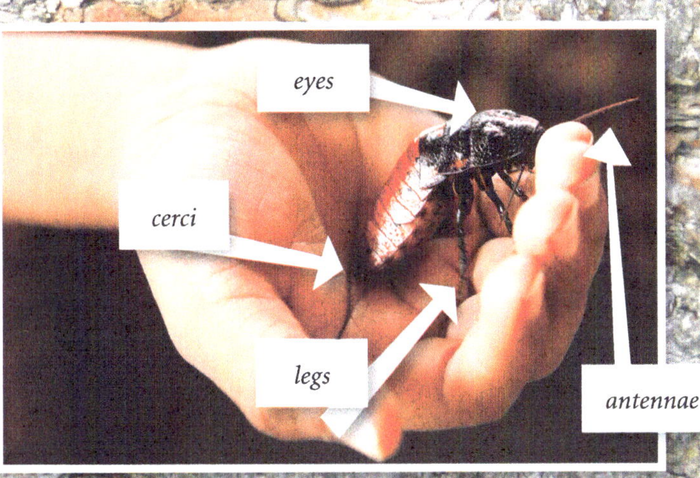

Dark Not Light

Madagascar hissing cockroaches don't like light and will only move around in the dark. Chuck's team placed dark red lights inside the enclosure so that they would move around.

> "IF IT WAS LIGHT, THE COCKROACHES WOULD HIDE AND THAT WOULD BE BORING FOR THE KIDS."
>
> CHUCK

A New Home

When the exhibit was finished, the 9000 cockroaches settled into their new home for a few weeks before people were allowed to visit. This gave the zoo staff enough time to make sure that the cockroaches were happy in their homes.

When the zoo is closed, the dark red lights are turned off and the cockroaches stop hissing and rest – until the zoo reopens again.

Chuck's Cockroach Story

Author Question:
Chuck, do you ever secretly return to a zoo you've designed?

Chuck's Answer:
Yes, and here's my favourite story. "A year after we finished the cockroach exhibit for the Lincoln Park Zoo in Chicago, I returned."

Chuck tells a story

"It was a quiet day in spring. I walked over to the cockroach exhibit. When I arrived, I watched a family with a young boy walk into the dark exhibit. I followed them inside. As our eyes adjusted to the darkness, I saw the young boy walk up to the cockroach exhibit window. He reached out in the darkness to touch the glass window but his hand landed on one of our plastic cockroaches!"

"Suddenly the boy jumped back in fright. He quickly realised that it wasn't real so he moved toward the exhibit window again. He looked in amazement at the thousands of cockroaches crawling on the other side of the glass."

"I was happy that this young boy didn't cry and run away – he felt safe enough to stay. As the cockroach exhibit designer, that was a great sight for me to see!"

Chuck Mayes

kids enjoy the cockroach exhibit

Animals' New Homes: An **Interview**

Author: Can zoo visitors see the animals as soon as they are put into their new homes?

Chuck: No. The zoo's animal carers like to wait up to eight weeks to make sure the animals are happy and that everything works well in their new home. When the zoo carers are satisfied that the animals are happy, the exhibit is opened to the public.

Author: How long does it take for animals to get used to their new homes?

Chuck: It can depend on the personality of the animal. Some animals take longer to get used to their new home than others. It may also depend on whether it is a single species' home or a mixed species' home.

For example, in a mixed species' aviary, birds may be added to their new home one at a time. This is less stressful for all the birds.

a rainbow lorikeet in an aviary

6 Amazing Aquariums

Sleek **Sea Lions** Swim

Chuck has designed many aquariums. His biggest challenge is to design a natural marine environment to support all the animals and plant life required in a marine ecosysytem.

Chuck works with many people who are experienced in designing and building aquariums. They also make sure that the construction is safe and strong.

Sea lions swim up to 40 kilometres an hour.

AQUARIUM MATERIALS

Imagine how many acrylic windows, plumbing fixtures, floor drains, wires and pipes are used to construct an aquarium. Once the aquarium is built, it is filled with thousands of litres of water and marine animals, such as sea lions, sharks and stingrays.

Everyone enjoys watching sea lions!

DO SEA LIONS CRY?

Sea lions may appear to cry, but they use their tear ducts to remove salt water from their eyes.

Sea lions can remain submerged for up to 40 minutes at a time!

A Close-Up **View** of **Sharks**

"Hey Mum, look at the shark's tail!"

"Yes! That back tail is called the caudal fin."

SHARK FINS

A shark has three kinds of fins to help it swim. There are the two dorsal fins on the shark's back and one pectoral fin under its body.

7 Discoveries in Zoos

Learn, **Touch** and **Dig**

Chuck enjoys designing educational exhibits for children at zoos and aquariums.

Experienced staff at zoos, museums and aquariums help children learn more about animals and their ecosystems.

Interactive learning sites provide a range of information about the zoo's animals.

Touch Tide Pools

One of Chuck's exhibits includes small tide pools. This is where children can get gentle finger hugs from living marine organisms, such as small fish, sea stars and sticky sea anemones.

Digging for fossils at the Junior Paleo Program – Utah Field House of Natural History Museum, USA.

"Hey, press that and we'll find out where the tigers are!"

At Oregon's Hatfield Marine Science Centre in the USA, children can touch animals in the tide pools and gather information for their projects.

Finding Fossils at a **Zoo!**

Everyone gets excited when they find fossils. So what are they? Fossils are the remains of living organisms, or their shapes in rock, that are between a few thousand and several millions of years old. But most living organisms decay and don't become fossils. Conditions have to be right for a fossil to form.

In some zoos, Chuck and his team have created exhibits where families can dig for fossils just like paleontologists.

Families dig for fossils at the Russia's Grizzly Coast exhibit at the Minnesota Zoo, USA.

The exhibit sign provides helpful information.

PALEONTOLOGISTS

A paleontologist is a person who studies life from prehistoric or geologic times in the form of fossils, such as plants and animals.

8 A Discussion: "Should We Allow Animals to Be Kept in Zoos?"

Today Jack and Mia, both nine years old, will discuss whether animals should be kept in zoos.

"FOR" the Topic

"Hello, my name is Jack. I agree with the topic. I think that we should allow animals to be kept in zoos."

"AGAINST" the Topic

"Hello, my name is Mia. I disagree with the topic. I think that we should not allow animals to be kept in zoos."

"FOR" the Topic

"Imagine not being able to go to zoos. By visiting zoos we learn more about animals and how to care for those that are endangered or threatened."

"AGAINST" the Topic

"I disagree. I have researched some zoos on the Internet that don't look after animals very well. We should leave animals in their natural environment."

"FOR" the Topic

"But people do not harm the animals in zoos."

"AGAINST" the Topic

"Maybe so, but we should travel to see the animals in the wild."

"FOR" the Topic

"Many families can't afford to travel to see animals in the wild. So most zoos build animal enclosures that are like their natural homes."

"AGAINST" the Topic

"People can see the animals on television documentaries and the Internet. The zoos' animal enclosures may look like their natural homes, but they are not!"

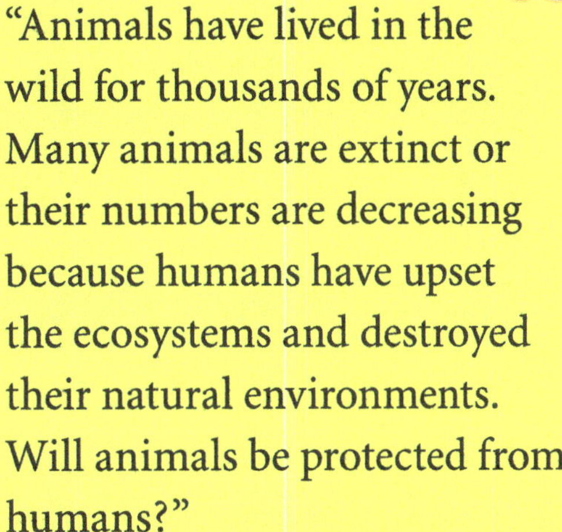

"FOR" the Topic

"Yes, we can see animals on television and the Internet but we learn more about animals in the safety of zoos where we can see them, smell them, hear their sounds and observe their habits."

"Zoos today design bigger and more natural environments to enable animals to live longer, healthier and happier lives."

"AGAINST" the Topic

"Animals have lived in the wild for thousands of years. Many animals are extinct or their numbers are decreasing because humans have upset the ecosystems and destroyed their natural environments. Will animals be protected from humans?"

"Zoos are not the answer!"

The Walrus **Decides**

Both Jack and Mia presented good arguments. But, in my opinion, animals should be allowed to be kept in zoos when they have:

- excellent care by animal experts
- large enclosures like their homes in the wild
- food like their natural diet in the wild
- a high standard of veterinary care.

Geography Feature

Top Zoos in the World

Chester Zoo: Chester, UNITED KINGDOM

This zoo is home to over 7000 animals, including some of the most endangered species on Earth.

Calgary Zoo: Calgary, CANADA

Children accompanied by an adult can stay overnight at the zoo for the "Dinosaurs After Dark Sleepover".

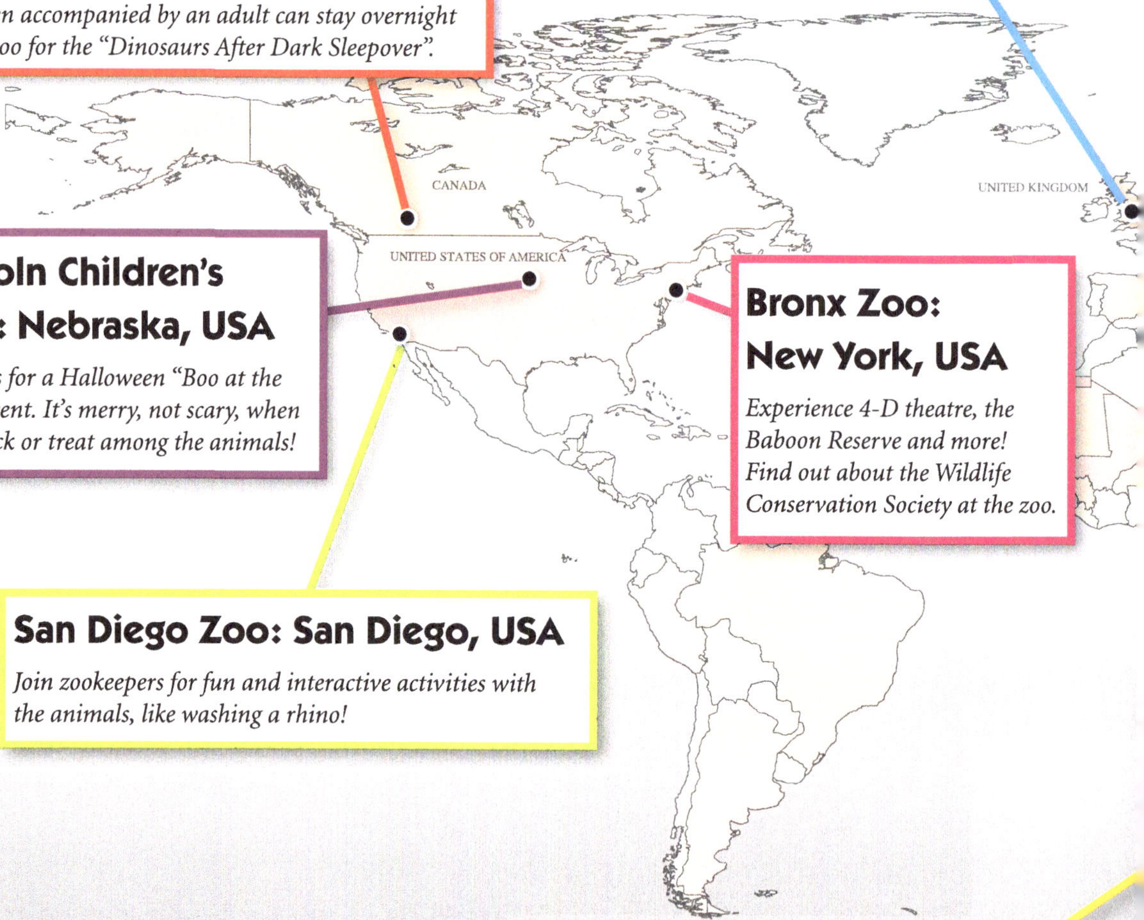

CANADA

UNITED KINGDOM

UNITED STATES OF AMERICA

Lincoln Children's Zoo: Nebraska, USA

Famous for a Halloween "Boo at the Zoo" event. It's merry, not scary, when kids trick or treat among the animals!

Bronx Zoo: New York, USA

Experience 4-D theatre, the Baboon Reserve and more! Find out about the Wildlife Conservation Society at the zoo.

San Diego Zoo: San Diego, USA

Join zookeepers for fun and interactive activities with the animals, like washing a rhino!

National Zoological Gardens: Pretoria, SOUTH AFRICA

Set up a tent and camp in the middle of the zoo!

Schönbrunner Zoo: Vienna, AUSTRIA

The oldest zoo in the world was founded in 1752. It has an Arctic Polarium featuring animals such as penguins and seals.

Ueno Zoological Gardens: Tokyo, JAPAN

The oldest zoo in Japan was founded in 1882. It includes a tea house that was built in the 17th Century.

Singapore Zoo: Singapore, REPUBLIC OF SINGAPORE

An open zoo where animals roam in natural-habitat enclosures.

Taronga Western Plains Zoo: Sydney, AUSTRALIA

Go to an overnight slumber party where you can hear roars and snores!

Pinnawela Elephant Orphanage: Kegalle, SRI LANKA

See the biggest herd of elephants (about 69) in the world.

Werribee Open Range Zoo: Melbourne, AUSTRALIA

Travel in an open vehicle to see animals close-up, such as lions, giraffes and zebras!

Auckland Zoo: Auckland, NEW ZEALAND

Go "backstage" and help the zookeepers feed the animals!

Index

Glossary

ecosystem	A group of living things, such as plants, animals and bacteria, that depend on each other for survival
far east Russia	The part of Russia that lies above Asia and west of Alaska
high-altitude	Very high up, such as on mountains or in the upper parts of the atmosphere
Northern Hemisphere	The northern half of a sphere, in this case Earth, lying above the equator
organisms	Living things, such as animals, plants, fungi and bacteria
poaching	Illegal hunting, or taking, of animals or plants
sanctuaries	Areas where animals are kept safe from harm and protected from predators
sewerage	Animal or human waste that is washed or flushed down drains